TULLY AND THE
SCARY DAY

Available in the Tales of Tully series

Tully's Life
This heart-warming story follows the journey of Tully from street dog to much-loved family pet, teaching young readers about the importance of kindness, understanding and hope.

Tully Takes Off!
Tully has arrived in her new home with her new grown-up, but she does not like it one bit! When Tully sees an opportunity to go back to her old life on the streets - the only life she has known up to now - she takes it with both paws. With a search underway, it is up to her new grown-up to work out what Tully needs and help get her safely home.

Tully and the Sad Day
Tully has woken up feeling grey and cloudy inside and she does not know what to do. She cannot help her big feeling because she does not know what it is. As her different feelings begin to work together in the wrong way, it is up to Tully's grown-up to help her to understand what she needs.

Go To Sleep Tully!
It is night time and Tully is tired, but she does not want to go to sleep. Her new grown-up knows that Tully is trying every trick she can to avoid going go to bed! With lots of adventures planned and Tully needing her rest, Tully's grown-up needs to find a way to help Tully learn to not be so worried about bedtime.

Tully and the Midnight Feast
Tully is a newly-adopted dog settling in with her new grown-up. Since her arrival, her snacks have started mysteriously disappearing from the cupboard and appearing under her bed, she seems to have forgotten her manners, and there are days when she just cannot stop eating! Tully and her grown-up need to work together to help Tully with her worries about food.

Tully and the Scary Day
Tully has woken up feeling scared. She isn't really sure why, but today feels like a very scary day, and she just wants to hide. Tully's grown-up is thankfully there to help Tully manage her big feelings and see that the day is not so scary after all.

Don't Touch Tully!
Tully is settling in with her new grown-up. She has learned that the new grown-up is a safe person and she enjoys strokes and cuddles with them. Then Tully starts to meet new people, who want to show her how loved she is. Unfortunately, Tully doesn't feel the same about people she does not know and trust. It is up to Tully's grown-up to find a way to help Tully with her big feelings and to be Tully's voice, when she can't use hers.

Tully and the Tummy Ache
Tully has a tummy ache and it's making her feel quite grumpy. She doesn't want to eat or drink, and she can't get comfortable. Her tummy is sore and it's getting worse! Tully is in a toilet muddle. So, Tully and her grown-up work together to sort the muddle out and help Tully to cure her tummy ache.

Tully's Birthday
It's Tully's birthday, and her grown-up has planned a special day for her, but Tully doesn't feel like celebrating. As the day begins to unfold, so do Tully's big feelings. Tully doesn't know what to do about the big feelings, so she does a bad thing. Luckily, Tully's grown-up is there to help her feel better about herself, and enjoy the rest of her birthday.

Listen, Tully!
Tully does not always like to listen, especially when her grown-up is trying to stop her having fun. Tully decides that instead of listening, she can be in charge. But when things start to go wrong, Tully and her grown-up need to work out how Tully can begin to find listening a little bit easier.

Tully and the Makeover
Tully has been having lots of fun playing in the mud, but now her grown-up says she has to have a bath. Oh dear! Tully is not sure she wants one of those. She is feeling a bit nervous about what is going to happen to her, but Tully's grown-up shows her that there is nothing to worry about. Having a bath is a good thing after all.

Tully and Vera
Tully has moved in with her new grown-up but she is missing her foster carer, Vera. Tully is struggling to understand why she had to leave, and whether it is okay to have big feelings about Vera. It is up to Tully's grown-up to try and help her to understand loss and endings and why, sometimes, they have to happen to make space for new beginnings.

Tully and the Chase
Tully loves to be chased. It gives her a feeling of excitement which starts off as being fun, but one day the excited feeling suddenly and very quickly becomes a feeling which is too big. Instead of feeling excited, Tully starts to feel scared. Tully and her grown-up need to work out how they can play Tully's exciting game without it becoming a bit too much for her, and causing a muddle.

Tully at Christmas
Things are starting to feel a bit different in Tully's house and all around outside. Tully's grown-up looks different, strange lights are appearing everywhere and people have started putting their gardens indoors! Tully is not sure what to make of this thing called Christmas – she just wants everything to stay the same. What can Tully's grown-up do to make Christmas-time a nicer time for both of them?

Tully Goes on Holiday
Tully has gone on a holiday with her grown-up. After a difficult start, things seem to be going well. But when the fairground opens up, with all its flashing lights, loud music and food smells, Tully's big feelings get the better of her, making her want to run. And she does! Tully's grown-up needs to find her in time to show her that holidays can be fun after all.

Tully and the New Rules
Tully likes lots of things about living in a house with her grown-up, but one thing she really doesn't like is all the rules! Tully thinks the rules are all very boring and her grown-up must want to stop her from having fun. One day Tully breaks her least favourite rule, and something bad happens. Tully doesn't know what to do! Can Tully's grown-up get to the bottom of this muddle so it doesn't happen again?

Tully and the Scary Day

TALES OF TULLY

Jess van der Hoech

Trauma Tools
& Training

Acknowledgements

As always, to my trusted editor Sarah Ogden for all that you do to make these books come to life. I will never fully know what goes on behind the scenes, but it is a joy to work alongside you on these projects. Thank you.

Thank you to my supervisor Linda Hoggan for your continued support, encouragement, discussion and much-welcomed feedback on this series. I learn so much from you and the knowledge I have gained form our conversations has been invaluable across my practice, the books and now this series. Thank you.

Thank you to Laura Benham, for your support in giving me feedback, the searching questions, your friendship and of course, the countless conversations about dogs, the content of which has become quite useful! Thank you.

To the children and families who I meet in my therapy room, from whom I have learned more about hope and healing than any course could ever teach me. Your input, ideas, questions and answers are so valuable to me and I will be forever grateful. Thank you.

Preface

The *Tales of Tully* series is based on the adoption of an ex street dog from Bosnia who came to live with me in September 2023. Watching her try to settle and adapt from everything she had previously known to fit in with a new way of life began to present a number of ideas as to how to communicate such difficulties that can be experienced, to others who are in the process of adopting or who have adopted children. The aim of the series is to provide an opportunity to explore different situations, circumstances, feelings and experiences, finding new ways of communicating and understanding each other, through the voice of Tully.

In order to survive early trauma, the lower 'survival' regions of the brain are activated more than the higher 'thinking' regions of the brain. Children who have lived through an experience which was not safe and therefore imposed a high level of threat to their survival, have a much stronger survival system. This was turned up at the time of the experience in order to cope with it, and it can be difficult to turn it down again when the threat has passed.

Even though the child may logically know that their circumstances are different now, this logic is not always enough to stop the brain from functioning in the same way it has done in the past. Some days can still feel very scary, even if there is no apparent reason for that to be so.

For children who have lived in a state of fear, life needs to be predictable in order to cement the feeling of safety that they now require in order to begin to heal. *Tully and the Scary Day* can start to help these children to make sense of why they feel scared, and how to start to heal this with the help of their safe grown-ups.

When Tully first came to live with me in the UK, she spent weeks in a state of fear; she was an exceptionally fearful dog. She needed to learn how our house 'worked'. Noises that are part of day to day life – the doorbell or the ping of the microwave for example – would cause her to immediately enter a hyper-aroused state, her body shaking as she tried to make sense of the world around her now.

I noticed that she would choose her bed on better days, the crate covered with a blanket on days that were trickier, and behind the sofa was reserved for the scariest days. I came to learn that when she was in her crate or behind the sofa, she needed to know that no one would try and get her out from there. These were her safe places and I would always be there when she decided to come out, but I would wait for her to decide when she was ready to do so.

I have had to become the most predictable person she has ever known in order to create that sense of safety. Whenever I come home from being out, as I walk through the door I call "Hello Tully, beautiful girl," I sit beside her, she smells my hand to make sure it's me, I rub her chest, her chin then stroke her head – always in that order. While this may seem like an extreme intervention for a dog, I have no doubt that taking actions like this, on repeat, every single time, has helped us to create the bond we now have.

When creating a secure attachment with a child, the advice would be the same. The grown-up needs to become the most predictable person in the child's world. Having a safe place in the home for the child to go when they need it, being greeted in the same way each time having been apart, having comfortable clothes that are better suited for the 'prickly' days when sensory input feels too much – all are ways of not only helping the child and grown-up to connect, but also to help the child begin to recognise and make little plans for their own big feelings.

How to use this book

First and foremost, ensure that both you and the child are well-regulated and comfortable when you begin to read Tully's story. Make sure you choose a time when you are unlikely to be interrupted. The child may like a soother, a favourite or fidget toy, a drink or something to suck or chew to help them to stay regulated.

If the child is calm, then begins to try and distract or move away from the reading, make a note of what they have just heard in the text. It is very likely that they will have just provided you with some valuable information about something that they cannot tolerate or want to avoid for now.

The questions have been designed not only to explore the internal world of the child, but to help to develop a common language between the child and adult who are using this book together. The child cannot get the answers to the questions incorrect. Their interpretation of the thoughts and feelings Tully is having may provide some very significant information about the child's own thoughts and feelings. The child may want to expand the answers to talk about themselves and may even be able to make comparisons between Tully's feelings and their own.

Tully and the Scary Day

It was a wet and windy morning and Tully's grown-up had called her three times so far to get out of bed. Tully did not want to get up. She had a bad feeling about today, so she decided to stay in bed.

What might a 'bad feeling' be?

What might be giving Tully a bad feeling?

"Come on Tully! Up you get," her grown-up said. Tully did not want to get up, but she did not want her grown-up to be cross with her either.

Tully was in a muddle. She thought about what she should do. Eventually she decided that she would get up from her bed and go and lie on the sofa instead. She did not want to go outside today. Today felt like a scary day.

Where might Tully feel scary feelings in her body?

How could Tully's grown-up know that Tully is feeling like this?

When Tully was a puppy, she had lived as a street dog in Bosnia. This meant that she had lived on her own without a person to keep her safe. Lots of Tully's days had been scary and even though she was not a street dog anymore, sometimes Tully's body still had the scary feelings.

Tully felt jumpy and restless. The scary feeling inside her made her want to move. Except she did not want to move because it felt too scary. Tully felt stuck.

The postman came to the door with a parcel and rang the doorbell. Even though Tully had seen him walking up the garden path, the noise of the doorbell sounded extra loud today and it made Tully jump.

What might Tully be thinking?

What does Tully need?

Tully's grown-up wanted to take Tully for her daily exercise and so put her harness on her. The harness felt tight and uncomfortable today, so Tully wriggled out of it and went and hid behind the sofa.

Tully liked it behind the sofa, so she stayed there for a while. She felt like no one could get to her there and it made her feel safe. After a while, Tully started to doze off.

Suddenly, there was a huge crash from the kitchen. Tully did not know what the noise was and it frightened her. Tully could not remember where she was. She felt like she was a street dog in Bosnia by herself again, and the scary feeling came back bigger than ever.

What might Tully do next?

Tully's body wanted to run but she could not move, she was stuck! She felt confused and in a big muddle. Just then, Tully heard something familiar.

It was the sound of her grown-up singing a little song. The grown-up often sang that song to Tully. It helped Tully to remember where she was and that her grown-up was still around. Her grown-up sang the song every morning when Tully woke up, every night when Tully went to bed and when Tully was hiding.

Why might Tully's grown-up sing the same song lots of times?

How does this make Tully feel?

Tully's grown-up came to see her and looked at her behind the sofa. "Sorry Tully, the big crash was just me dropping a pan. Everything is okay."

Tully's grown-up never tried to get Tully out from behind the sofa but would sometimes sit where Tully could see them. The grown-up knew that Tully went behind the sofa when she needed to feel safe, on days like today that felt very scary.

Why does Tully's grown-up do this?

Does Tully like this?

As Tully began to feel safe again behind the sofa, she was able to start to have a little think. She remembered where she was with her safe grown-up, in her safe house. She knew the noises sounded loud because today felt like a scary day. Tully thought of all the things that made her feel safe.

What are some things that might make Tully feel safe?

What are the things that make you feel safe?

As Tully began to feel safer and safer, she decided that she wanted to come out of her hiding place and go for a walk. Her skin still felt prickly and she did not want her big harness for big walks on. Tully knew that there was another lead that attached to her collar that her grown-up used for their little walks. Tully went into the kitchen and stood under the peg with the smaller lead hanging from it, to let her grown-up know what she wanted.

Why might Tully want a little walk today instead of a long one?

Tully and her grown-up went for their walk. Her grown-up kept her close and as they walked, the grown-up reminded Tully of all the ways she was safe now. Tully's grown-up told her she was very brave for coming on the walk today.

Tully and her grown-up know that even though Tully is safe now, some days might still feel a bit scary and that is okay. Tully knows that her grown-up will always help her to make those days feel safe again.

What are the things that your grown-ups do to help you to feel safe?

About the author

Jess van der Hoech is a qualified therapist who has spent the last ten years studying and working with the impact of developmental trauma and, in particular, the assessment and treatment of children and adolescents with complex trauma and dissociation.

As well as supporting birth families, Jess works with looked-after and adopted children and families, using skills in attachment-focused therapy and therapeutic parenting techniques.

Jess is a supervisor, trainer and motivational speaker with a passion for writing therapeutic books that are accessible to children and families to help with the healing process and to increase awareness in the impact of trauma.

Also by Jess van der Hoech

What A Muddle (2016) ISBN 978 18381987 0 1 (Co-authored with Renée Potgieter Marks)
An interactive, practical workbook designed to help children who have difficulties with emotional regulation to begin to understand what is happening in their bodies. A variety of activities throughout the book enable the child to start to explore these ideas through the story of Sam, while gently encouraging them to begin to verbalise their own experiences. Carrying out the physical exercises in the book can promote changes in emotional regulation. The text is written in a child-friendly, gender-neutral style, and is easy to understand for parents, carers and practitioners alike. For children aged 4-12.

These Three Words (2018) ISBN 978 18381987 5 6
Also available as an e-book. A unique therapeutic novel for teenagers with the aim of linking together the feelings, emotions and behaviours connected to anxiety, with some of the therapeutic tools that can be used in order to enable better self-regulation, increased confidence and different ways of thinking. The book is equally valuable to parents of teenagers with anxiety, giving them an insight and understanding into some of the issues that may be affecting their child, and potentially opening up a line of communication and a way forward between parent and teen.

These Three Words: The Journal (2019) ISBN 978 18381987 2 5
A thought-provoking and hands-on workbook, combining a series of practical exercises and tools designed to assist teenagers who are struggling with the symptoms of anxiety. Addressing the anxious responses in both brain and body, this journal provides the reader with the opportunity to discover therapeutic coping techniques and learn how to apply them to their own personal problem areas, before committing to a twenty-eight-day practice to promote good emotional regulation and reduced anxiety. The journal can be used alongside the therapeutic novel These Three Words, or as a standalone workbook, and it is suitable for use by the teenage reader on their own, with a parent, or in a group.

Beastie, Baby and the Brand-New Mummy (2022) ISBN 978 18381987 3 2 and *Beastie, Baby and the Brand-New Daddy (2022) ISBN 978 18381987 4 9*
A therapeutic story that looks at the external signs of pathological dissociation in a child. Dolly's story helps children who have experienced early trauma to begin to understand, in a very simple way, what dissociation is and why it has happened in their internal world. Tools and techniques are included within the story that parents and caregivers can use to assist the child in the first stages of their healing process. Beautiful illustrations on every page enhance the story of Dolly, and help the reader to relate to the events that happen, to notice the methods Dolly has developed to manage her feelings, and to think about what is happening in their own internal world. For children aged 4-12

Printed in Great Britain
by Amazon